To..

From ....

MR. MEN   LITTLE MISS
MR. MEN™ LITTLE MISS™ © THOIP (a SANRIO company)

Mr. Men Little Miss You Are Brilliant © 2020 THOIP (a SANRIO company)
Printed and published under license from Penguin Random House LLC
Published in Great Britain by Egmont UK Limited
2 Minster Court, 10th floor, London EC3R 7BB

ISBN 978 1 4052 9665 6
70781/001
Printed in Italy

Stay safe online. Egmont is not responsible for content hosted by third parties.

Egmont takes its responsibility to the planet and its inhabitants very seriously.
We aim to use papers from well-managed forests run by responsible suppliers.

MR. MEN
LITTLE MISS

YOU ARE BRILLIANT

Roger Hargreaves

You are never too small to make a big impact.

Whether you shout from the rooftops …

Or go about things in a much quieter way ...

Don't let anyone label you to stop you being heard.

You can achieve amazing things by following your heart.

Use your talents to make a mark.

But have courage to face your fears
as you're braver than you realise.

And stronger than you think.

Believe in yourself

and

you can

overcome

any obstacle.

And never underestimate
the power of kindness.

Have hope for the world we're building together.

You have the right to be free and happy.

But it's also ok to be sad as those feelings show you care.

Speak out when
something is
not right.

Harness your emotions to help you shape the world.

There is only one you.

No one can define how big you dream ...

Or how far you go . . . . . .

Brilliance
is found in
all shapes and
colours and ages.

So go on, surprise everyone with what you can achieve.

You are brilliant!

I AM BRILLIANT

I am really good at ..Climbing Helping cook..........

....

I was brave when I ....

....

I was kind when I ....

....

I am proud that I ....

....

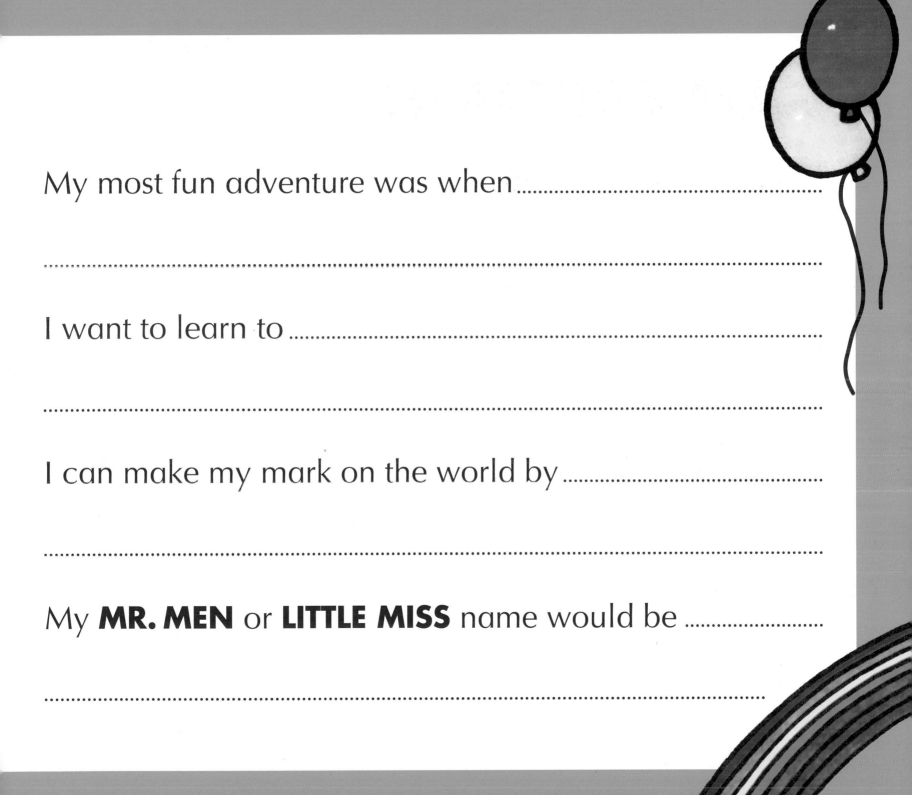

My most fun adventure was when ....

....

I want to learn to ....

....

I can make my mark on the world by ....

....

My **MR. MEN** or **LITTLE MISS** name would be ....

....

This is a picture
of me being brilliant:

by ....

aged ....